The Party

The Party

David McPhail

Little, Brown and Company

Boston   Toronto   London

COME TO MY **PARTY.**
IM all SO IN ViTing
ANAiMLS
AT
MY HOUSE

With thanks to the entire First Grade/Readiness Class
at the Wentworth School, Portsmouth, New Hampshire

To Kolya and Andreas
and their father,
Brother Jack

Copyright © 1990 by David McPhail

First Edition

Library of Congress Cataloging-in-Publication Data

McPhail, David M.
    The party/by David McPhail.
      p. cm.
    Summary: A boy's stuffed animals come to life one night and help
him have a party, to which his sleepy father is invited.
    ISBN 0-316-56330-7
    [1. Parties – Fiction.   2. Animals – Fiction.   3. Toys – Fiction.
4. Fathers and sons – Fiction.]   I. Title.
PZ7.M2427Par   1990
[E] – dc20   89-49297
                                       CIP
                                       AC

Joy Street Books are published by Little, Brown and Company (Inc.).

10 9 8 7 6 5 4 3 2 1

WOR

Published simultaneously in Canada
by Little, Brown & Company (Canada) Limited

Printed in the United States of America

It is nighttime.
We are planning a party –
my animal friends and me.

The party is just about to begin
when my father comes in to read us a story.

But right at the most exciting part...

… he falls asleep.

"We can't have a party now!" says Bear.

"We'll have to wake him up," I say.

We push and we poke, but my father doesn't even stir.

We try tickling him, but my father keeps right on sleeping.

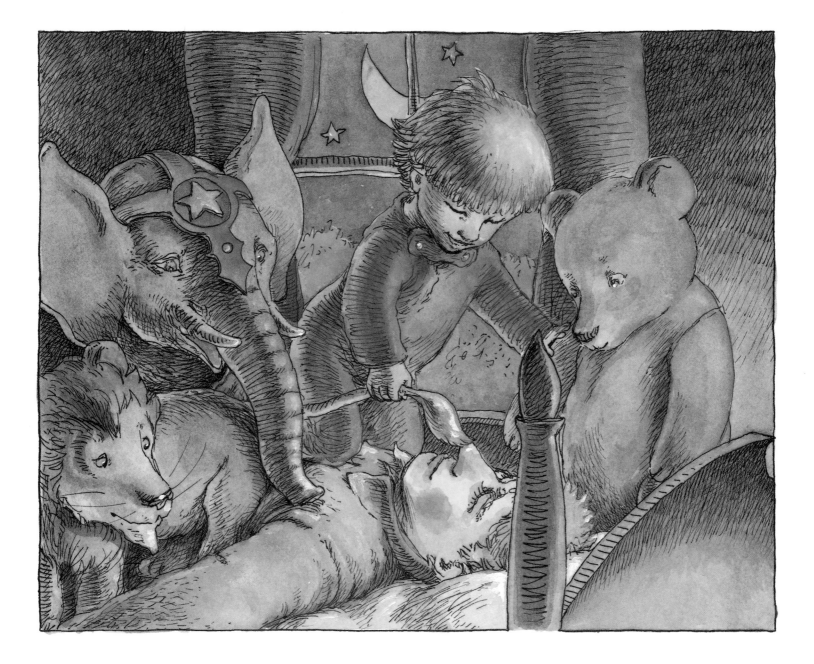

"We'll have a party anyway!" I tell my friends.

And we do.
We blow up balloons.
The ones that Bear blows up are so full of hot air
that we can hang on to them and float
around the room.
When we are over the bed we let go...
and BOUNCE!

After that we take a ride on my electric train.
"Duck, everybody!" I yell.
"We are going through a tunnel!"

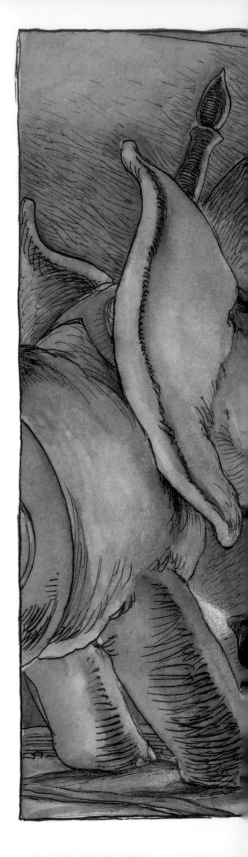

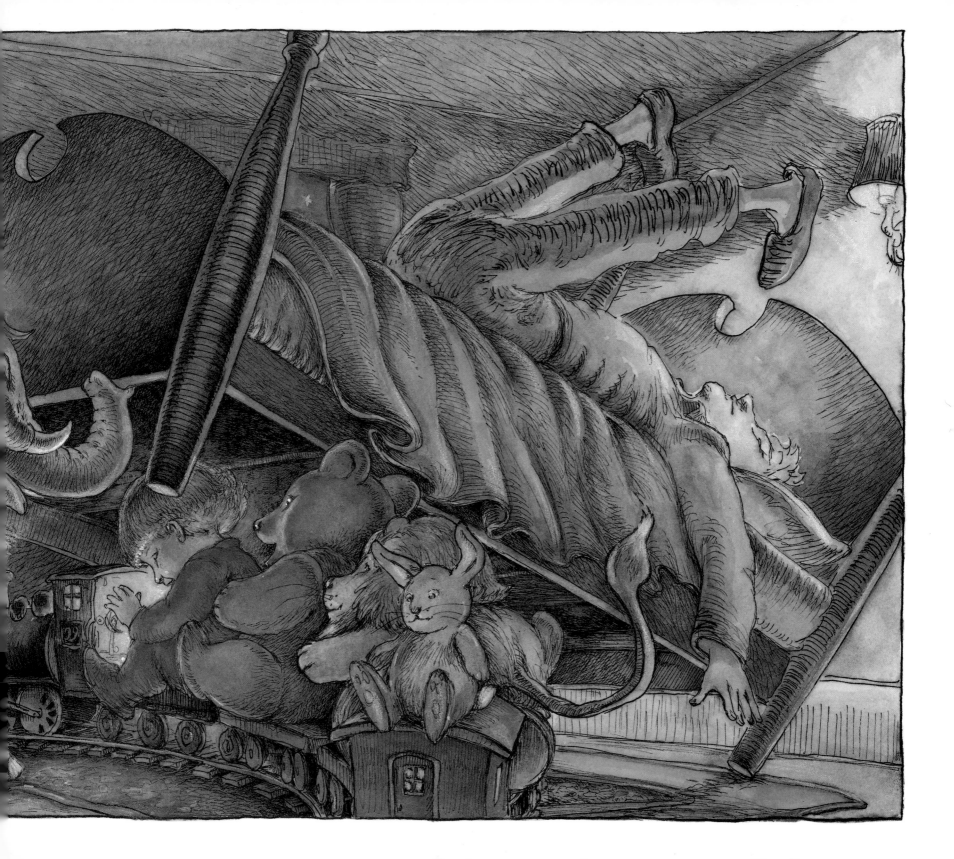

We make music and dance all around.
Bear is getting hungry.
"What's a party without food?" he asks.

So we go down to the kitchen for something to eat.

My father comes, too.

In the kitchen we help ourselves to whatever
we can find.

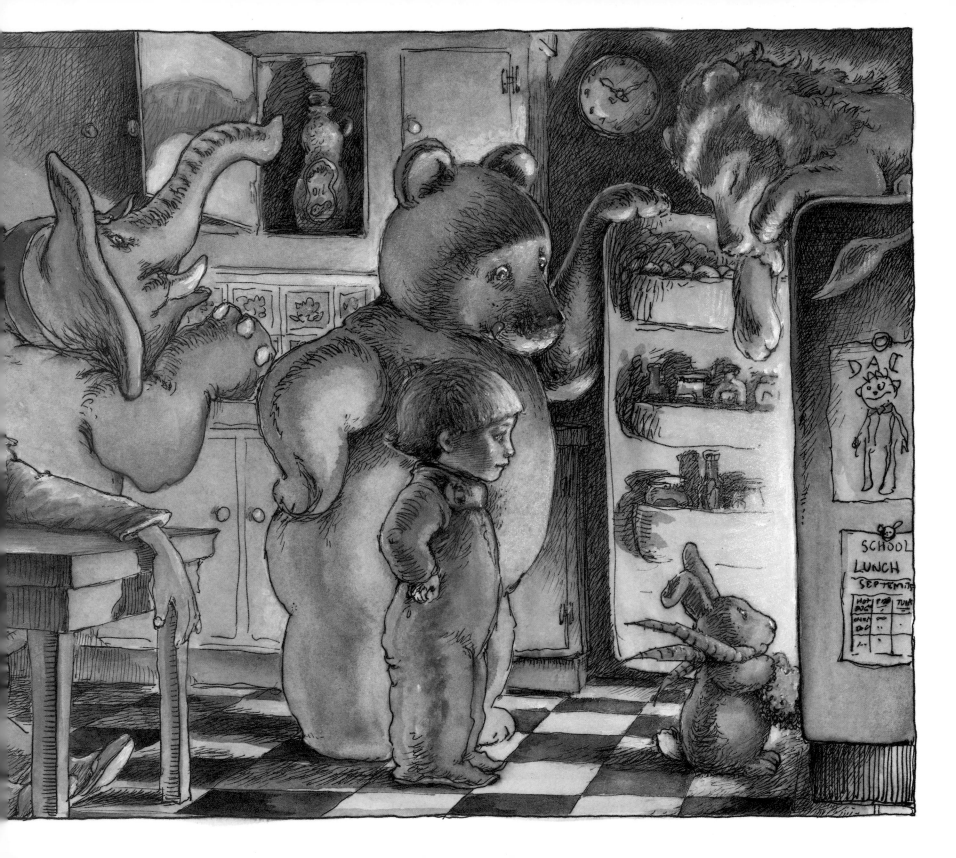

I make sandwiches for everybody.

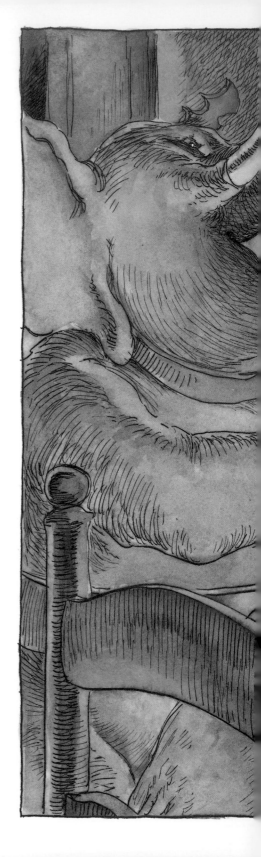

While we are eating, I hear my mother call my father.
"Are you coming to bed, dear?" she asks.
"Quick!" I say. "We've got to get back upstairs!"

It isn't easy.

But we finally make it.

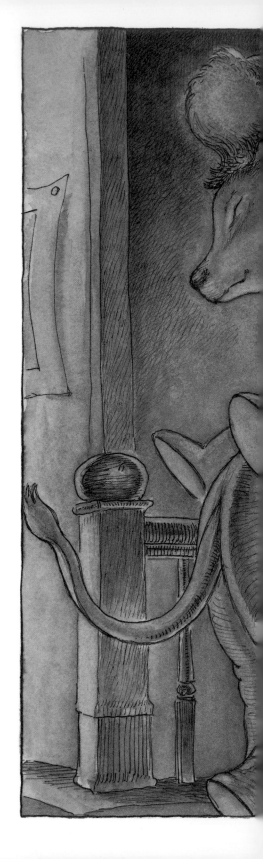

We stand my father up and give him a little push.

"Good night, Dad," I whisper.
"There you are, dear," says my mother.
"Were you having a snack?"

We quietly close the door.
"What shall we do now?" I ask.
"Well," said Bear, "I'm still hungry..."

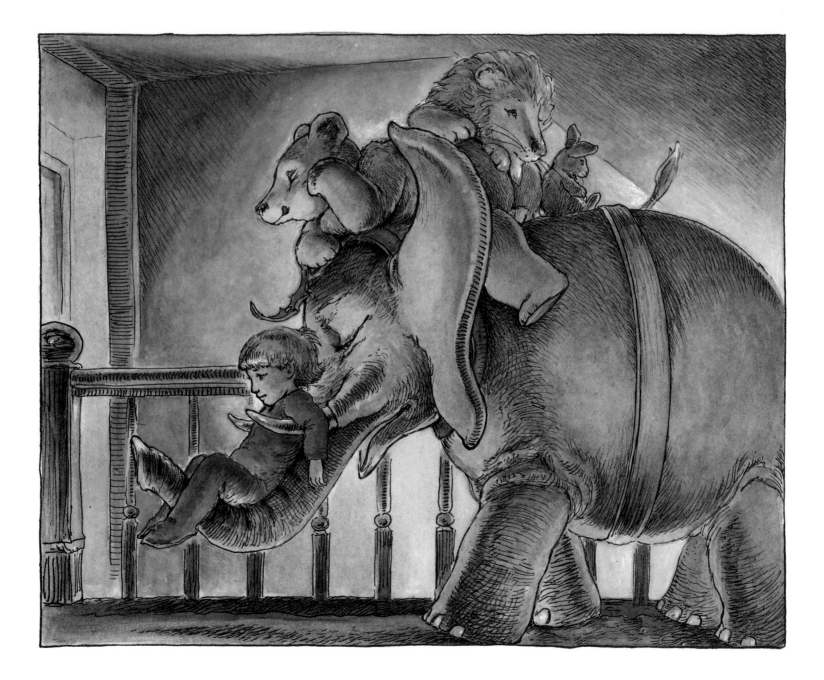